When ⌐
he fir̄... ̄ ...one, a....
nothing but a cheap instant camera. Then out of
the sunlight appears a girl in a scarlet dress . . .

Sutira and her little brother take Flash home.
The people of her village have never met a
photographer—never seen a photo—but
photography is the kind of magic everyone has
a use for.

Flash has only ten pictures left in his camera.
How can he best use them to make his new
friends smile?

Smile!

Other books by Geraldine McCaughrean
for older readers

Forever X
Gold Dust
The Kite Rider
A Little Lower than the Angels
A Pack of Lies
Plundering Paradise
The Stones Are Hatching
Stop the Train
Not the End of the World
The White Darkness
Cyrano
Peter Pan in Scarlet

Smile!

Geraldine McCaughrean

Illustrated by Ian McCaughrean

OXFORD
UNIVERSITY PRESS

For Flash

OXFORD
UNIVERSITY PRESS

Great Clarendon Street, Oxford OX2 6DP

Oxford University Press is a department of the University of Oxford.
It furthers the University's objective of excellence in research, scholarship,
and education by publishing worldwide in

Oxford New York
Auckland Cape Town Dar es Salaam Hong Kong Karachi
Kuala Lumpur Madrid Melbourne Mexico City Nairobi
New Delhi Shanghai Taipei Toronto

With offices in
Argentina Austria Brazil Chile Czech Republic France Greece
Guatemala Hungary Italy Japan Poland Portugal Singapore
South Korea Switzerland Thailand Turkey Ukraine Vietnam

Oxford is a registered trade mark of Oxford University Press
in the UK and in certain other countries

British Library Cataloguing in Publication Data
Data available

ISBN 978-0-19-271961-4

7 9 10 8

Printed in Great Britain by Cox & Wyman Ltd,
Reading, Berkshire

Flash

Suddenly he was falling, and his life went past in small, square pictures, framed in the windows of the cockpit. There were his family; his house; his friends; his wedding; his dog. There were pictures of the Past and pictures of the Future, too—all the things he had meant to do and now never would: bridges, faces, dawns, and sunsets.

There were flames, as well, but they were not imaginary. They really were running their orange tongues over the glass, licking away the views, gobbling up the sky. Flash would have liked to bid someone goodbye, but he was all alone in the plane.

The next he knew, the windows were full of desert: red gulches and yellow valleys and salt-white lakes. The landscapes were so beautiful and so strange that Flash wanted to capture them—trap them like rare, free-flying birds. He wanted to photograph them.

No time for developer and fixer. No time for darkrooms and prints. His hands closed around the only camera of any use to him.

Then the plane tilted and it was too late. The scenes framed in its windows flickered by too fast to focus upon. As a cinema film rattles free of its spool, so Flash's fall rattled to an end. The crashing aeroplane landed in a sea of grey-green trees, folding its wings upwards like a butterfly. Branches broke through the floor. Leaves burst into the cockpit. The glass windows crazed like eggshell. If Flash had not been thrown out through the shattering roof, his life would have finished then and there. The End.

He fell heels-over-heart into a clump of thorn bushes. Just once his eyelids blinked, like a camera shutter, and took in the sight of his aeroplane burning, raised aloft on the arms of three blazing trees. In his head, he titled the picture *Scorching the Sky*. Then his eyes closed and he returned to a darkroom empty of pictures or even of dreams.

Sutira and Olu

'Who are you?' he asked.

'That's not hard. I know that,' said the little girl. 'What I don't know is who you are.'

She was poking long, straight branches up the legs of his trousers, and Flash felt mildly annoyed to be woken only in time to be spit-roasted.

'Olu and I, we take you home,' said the girl. She had dusky, dusty skin the colour of milky tea, and a scarlet dress. Her long, ragged hair was dusty, too. It brushed Flash's face as she pushed the branches on through his shirt and out at the collar. Then she waved to the little boy to take his place by Flash's head.

When Flash realized what they were doing, he marvelled at their cleverness. Wonderful! That these primitive people should know, so young, how to transport an injured man across hostile wilderness. They balanced something on his stomach, then they both took hold of the ends of the two branches and lifted Flash clear of the ground.

All the buttons burst from his shirt and his head hit the ground with a thud. The camera on his stomach rolled down and smacked him in the face.

'I say to Olu, I say it won't work,' said the girl, sagging under the weight of his body and legs. Any moment now she would drop him.

'Perhaps I can walk,' said Flash, feeling his trousers begin to split.

And he found that he could. He was dizzy

and burned, and the sun was like a kettle of hot water being poured over his aching head. But if he put one foot in front of the other and counted all the flies he passed on the way, somehow he could manage to walk. The hardest thing was to tell which flies he had already counted and which were new arrivals. They all wanted to fly into his mouth.

'What is the box?' asked the girl, pointing.

'A camera,' said Flash. 'I'm a photographer. That's what I do. Photographs.'

'Ah!' said the girl. And there was something about the empty coffee swirl of her eyes that told him instantly: she had never seen either a camera or a photographer before.

They walked over ground as lined as an old man's skin. They walked over carpets of fleshy little plants that crackled under their feet like crabs. They walked over dead flies and the empty skins of snakes. 'A camera takes pictures,' he told them.

The girl turned on him a fierce glare, as if he had just confessed to being a thief. 'Can't take ours,' she said. 'We need them.'

The village lay at the head of a ravine. There were round huts with grass roofs. There were sheep like goats—or maybe goats like sheep. There were looms and cooking pots and a crude, open-air forge. There were women and children and old men.

'What have you brought us, Sutira?' asked the girl's mother, with only mild surprise, as if every day her children brought home such things as Flash. The rest of the village women turned from combing wool, weaving grasses, nursing their babies. Children came to stare. But to Sutira's mother went the honour of greeting the stranger, since her children had salvaged him.

None of these people had ever been to a city. No TV satellite had ever poured its pictures into their heads. Once, during some distant war, a fleet of armoured cars had driven by on the horizon, but so long before that they were talked of like chariots in a legend. To these people, aeroplanes were of no more concern than noisy birds flying too high to shoot. Now and then, from passing pedlars, they came by fancy goods such as T-shirts and washing-line, a rifle or a plastic flower. But as for cameras ...

'He has a camera? Yes, I have seen these.' The crowd parted reverently and made way for an old, old man, stooped and sun-shrivelled. He leaned heavily on a staff, and Flash guessed that he had probably been born with more fingers than he now owned. 'Sometimes, before the war, there were travellers. *Smile! Tchuck!* Men use these things like honey-traps to catch butterflies.'

'Butterflies, yes, or views or faces or moments . . . !' They fluttered into the photographer's aching head, behind his sore eyes: all the wonderful things that cameras could capture.

' . . . And these butterflies,' the old, old man interrupted. 'They are loosed again?'

And Flash realized that it was not *cameras* that were utterly unknown in this remote and lonely place: only the photographs that came out of them.

'Yes, yes! In fact I can show you!' he said and, without thinking, pointed the camera at Sutira and Olu. 'Smile!'

Tchuck.

An explosion of light. A switch had been

knocked in the crash: the flash came on by mistake. Sutira and Olu screwed shut their eyes. They rammed the heels of their hands into their eye sockets. Twenty faces flinched from the brightness.

Guns flash, and they knew guns.

The children's mother came at Flash, fists over her head. His first thought was for the camera and he turned his back to shield it. (A photographer always thinks of his camera first.) 'No! I . . .' he began, but Sutira and Olu had begun to cry loudly that they were blinded.

So he took off and ran. And behind him the whole village gave a roar and came after him.

Ten Shots at
Forever

He was burned and battered and bruised. His whole skeleton had been jangled by the crash. Instead of running, he could only hop and hobble lamely. The villagers overtook him like a swarm of bees. He raised his camera high above his head, out of their reach. It had already poked out a tongue of white card.

'Look! Look!' he shouted. *'Let me show you!'* And he tugged it free and held it out to them: his harmless, instant photograph of the children.

But an instant photo takes time to appear. The villagers were unimpressed. All they could see was a small white square of nothing at all. Those with hoes or sticks raised their weapons to strike.

So Flash pointed the fearful camera at them, turning round and round on the spot. Camera in one hand, photo in the other, he kept them at bay.

Meanwhile, second by second, grain by grain, the picture appeared; pale at first, then darker. Growing dizzy, Flash singled out Sutira's mother in the crowd and pushed the photo towards her. She gave a cry of fear and looked around for her children. How could they be here, trapped in this white square, unless they had been captured and shrunk and imprisoned? Finding them, she snatched them close, pressing their heads roughly against her body. Then her eyes fixed again on the photograph, its picture still growing clearer and clearer.

And Flash talked as if his life depended on it. 'It's not very good! I'm sorry. I could do better. I don't generally use these trashy cameras. This one was in my hand when the plane . . . With a proper camera—with a good lens and variable focus—I could do you a nice study! Handsome children. Pretty children! Those reds and browns. Instant prints are all very well, but if the subject moves . . . I only generally use these for reference. Take it. Take it! It's yours! Take it! The flash was a mistake. It took out too many shadows. A good portrait needs shadows. And a smile, of course. A smile is always better . . .'

Now everyone was trying to see what the mother could see—what had made her eyes so round, what had made her jaw drop. They crowded behind her, peeping over her shoulders, staring at the square of card in Flash's trembling hand.

Then Olu's quick brown fingers snatched it and he and his sister stared, too, at faces they had only seen before in polished metal or still pools of water. The silence was unnerving.

'I could take *your* photo!' Flash offered the

mother. 'Or yours! Or yours!' He glanced quickly at the back of the camera. 'I only have nine shots left, but I . . .'

He was talking to himself. The crowd of villagers had turned back down the path towards the old, old man. During the chase, he had not moved one step. He was too old to chase photographers or information or a new and exciting sight. He waited for all three to come to him. Respectfully, Sutira's mother showed him the photograph, and the two men regarded each other from a distance. *Do not run*, said the old man's look. *There is nowhere to run.*

'Speak,' said the old, old man to Sutira and Olu. Promptly neither child could think of anything to say. They shuffled their feet and remained silent. 'Say a prayer!' commanded the old man. So Sutira and Olu prayed, and while they did so, the old man nodded, satisfied. The children were complete, inside and out—could still speak and think and had not lost their souls to the camera. (He had not expected any such thing, but it was just as well to check.) Raising one frail hand, hooking one bony finger, he summoned the man who had fallen from the sky.

But the sun was hot on Flash's head. The flies were trying to climb in at his ears and nose and eyes as well as his mouth. He sank down to his knees and then, laying his camera carefully aside, lay down on his face in the dirt, too weary to care what Fate held in store for him.

By evening, the photograph of Sutira and Olu had pride of place in their mother's house. Pinned to a strip of cloth, it hung from the roof, safe from insects. The hut was crowded, and neighbours queued at the door to view the photo. They wanted to see the Sutira who would stay ten for ever, the Olu whose face would always be cheeky-bright.

They stared, too, at the stranger lying on a mattress on the floor and at the box beside his head. He did not amaze them as much as the photograph did. They all knew that, every so often, God sends a stranger to call. Strangers are a blessing (so long as they don't shoot your children). So they gave him a liquor the colour of sprouts that took away his pain and fluffed out his thoughts like newly washed hair. They all hoped to have the honour of sharing a meal with him, if he did not die of his injuries first . . . but then that too lay in God's hands. No, strange as Flash seemed, in his denim trousers and shell-silk flying jacket, it was his photograph that held them spellbound. The forever-children; the instant work-of-art; the mirage that had somehow set hard and been peeled off the air.

It was very early morning when the old, old man called. He had waited until all the visitors were gone. Now he placed the foot of his staff hard by Flash's head and teetered unsteadily over him, examining his face.

'Why do you waste this on children? Great magic should be for great uses.'

'It's not mag—' began Flash, but stopped. How could he say that photography was not magic? Ever since childhood it had held him in its spell. A photograph can stop time. It can capture Now like a snowflake and keep it from melting away. It is a Memory pasted on to cardboard.

It is proof.

'I have nine shots left,' Flash told the Village

Elder. 'You are great in wisdom, sir. You tell me what to photograph and I will do it.'

The old man shrugged and pushed out his bottom lip. In his long life, he had heard flattery plenty of times before. 'Everyone will have his idea, her idea,' he said. 'I do the wisest thing of all. I let *you* choose. Nine pieces of magic. You choose.'

At the door, on his way out, he turned and added: 'There is the cow, of course.'

The Cow

It was a pleasant cow with an agreeable face, but it was just a cow. It was thin, too. Any Guernsey or Jersey standing in an English field would have put it to shame. There were cankers on its lumpy knees and, just by looking, Flash could count its ribs as easily as the bars on a xylophone. Once he had had a bicycle with handlebars just the same shape as those horns.

And yet they brought him this cow as if it were some priceless Arab stallion triumphant from winning the Derby.

'It's a cow,' said Flash stupidly, watching the cow drop dung at his feet. Then he thought: *Perhaps it's sacred. Perhaps these people believe cows are holy.* 'Fine cow,' he said more tactfully.

'Once, before the drought, we had ten-and-seven,' said the Village Elder. (Standing patting the cow's neck, Sutira seemed hardly to believe this. Such wealth could not be possible.) 'One by one they all died. We have not had a cow in this village for many, many years. Our women have worked far into the night. They have worked in the sleeping midday to make the liquor and lanka to trade. Last week we bought this beast. Now there will be milk again for the children. Dung to make the ground fertile. God is good.'

From all around came the harsh, cracking drumbeat of women beating with stones on strips of tree-bark. Metre by metre, coil by hank, they beat the bark into strands of fibre: a sort of raffia from which they made ropes and mats and ornamental braids. From every doorway hung nets of fruit dripping, drop by tedious drop, into bowls and pots. It was the liquor they had given Flash; liquor they had been making to trade for another cow.

'Of course I will photograph your cow,' said Flash, picking up the camera.

But first the cow had to be made presentable. So the children picked flowers to twine round her horns and the women washed her tail and fetched woven braids to hang across her flanks. When they stood her side-on to the camera, she looked as good as any painting by George Stubbs in the National Gallery.

'No,' said the magician with the box of marvels. 'Not like that.'

The cow and Flash looked each other over, sized each other up. Flash could see himself reflected in the big, liquid eyes.

The ladies of the village murmured their bewilderment. With the cow *facing* him, how would he show the rosy udders? How could he show the ribbons in her tail?

Flash still felt as unwell as if a herd of cows had stampeded over him. He had to set his feet wide apart to keep his balance. He shook his aching head. The cow shook her head, too, loosing a cloud of flies, making her big ears crack. *I know,* the cow seemed to say. *This sun on the top of the head: it can be very tiresome.*

'Smile!' said Flash, and though cows' faces are not built for smiling, it seemed to Flash that the tilt of the head was at least jaunty.

Tchuck!

From every side, beads rattled and hair splashed and hot arms and elbows jostled him, as Flash flicked the photo-card to and fro between his fingers. It looked as if he was coaxing the picture out of his fingertips and on to the white square of cardboard. He knew it. He enjoyed playing the magician: Maker of Pictures.

Second by second, grain by grain, the cow emerged, as if through the fog of an English meadow: a big nose, huge ears pink from the sunlight shining through them. There were the cankers on her bony front knees. There were her flowery horns, her miserably narrow chest. With her head so huge in the foreground, her body could hardly be seen—only two brown flanks ballooning out ridiculously to either side of the head. The back legs were not even visible.

The women stared at the odd creature in the photograph: the huge-headed, two-legged creature with sunlit ears and

bulging sides. Only then did Flash get the smile he had asked for.

'From the side you can't see, you see,' he said. 'The most important thing of all.'

Unless he had photographed the cow in

this way—head-on—the full splendour of
the village's treasured possession would not
have shown. From the side, you see, you
cannot tell that a cow has a calf inside her.

The Warriors

Flash started up out of a deep sleep. The women had given him more of that bitter liquor the colour of sprouts. It had taken away all his pain, but also made his dreams too big for his head, his arms too long for him to reach his hands. He could not remember where he was or why. Now there were men banging on the clay walls of the hut, sending spurts of dust flying about indoors.

'The warriors are home,' said Sutira.

This was not, of course, a village of women and old men, mothers and children. In the early morning, its young men came home. They brought with them a wild pig, a

47

lizard, some kind of large chicken, and all three seats out of the crashed aeroplane. Hearing tell of a stranger—a young man—arriving while they were gone, they surrounded Sutira's hut and banged on it with the butts of their rifles.

Quite calmly, Sutira rolled off her mattress and got to the door ahead of her brother.

'One by one you can come in,' she told the growl of voices outside. 'You first, cousin.'

So Sutira's cousin ducked in at the door—a boy so big and blustering that he seemed to be putting on the hut like a shirt rather than just entering. Sutira put a small hand into his and led him over to the photograph, explaining, describing, storytelling. She pointed out Flash, too, but only as she might a piece of second-hand furniture. She made light of him. Not much of a man. Not much of an event. Not much of a warrior. Simply a fool of a magician.

The warrior glared at Flash, and Flash stared blearily back, trying to remember why his mouth was underneath his nose and how his knees had been threaded on to his legs without taking off his feet.

'Tell about the pictures,' Sutira instructed him.

Flash tried to speak, but his mouth was full of skunks or cotton reels. He spread the fingers of both hands trying to signify the eight shots remaining in his instant camera. It was left to Sutira and her little brother to explain about the camera, the square of white card, the cow, and the possibility of portraits.

Still outside the hut, the other warriors listened. When they could not picture what she was talking about, they pushed their faces in at the door, scowling and glaring and waving their rifles idly at Flash. When at last they understood, they aimed their guns more enthusiastically, jabbing them towards his face, demanding, 'Me!'

'Me!'

'Me! Now!'

Flash put his hands high over his head. His brain, though still unable to count, told him there were already more than eight warriors in the hut. Some would be disappointed. None looked as if he would take kindly to disappointment.

Sutira's strident little voice broke through the din. 'Of course. He paints only best warrior!'

Ten minutes later, the argument had moved outside. Thirteen young men were scuffling and pushing, shouting and brawling. Some had wives, and those wives were in the hut instead, yelling their husbands' praises at Flash, trying to shout each other down.

'Why don't I photograph them all? In a group?' he kept saying but nobody was listening. The idea had taken root that the magician was going to photograph the best young man in the village. Now each warrior was bent on proving himself best. Olu ran to and fro with messages for the photographer.

'They fight each other till only one is standing!' Olu said.

'No!' said Flash. 'The camera does not want to photograph a man with torn ears and a broken nose!'

'They go hunt and you paint who brings the largest kill.'

'No!' said Flash, picturing the hut filled to the roof with dead lizards. 'The camera does not like meat.'

'They cut themselves and who cut deepest . . .'

'No!' said Flash. 'No! No! No! Definitely not.'

'They walk over hot coals . . .'

For a moment, the photographic appeal of thirteen handsome young men walking over glowing embers was seriously tempting. Then Flash pulled himself together. 'Say to the warriors: the camera will know the best man when it sees him!'

The noise outside sank to a nervous murmur. Flash uncrossed his legs and rose with as much dignity as he could muster. The wives parted to make way for him as he walked out-of-doors holding the camera in front of him like frankincense on his two flat hands.

'Draw a circle, Olu,' he said, and the boy followed behind him, dragging a stick through the soft dirt, etching a circle three metres wide. 'Let every man who wishes the camera to look him over stand in the circle!'

Like thirteen Santas jostling to get down one chimney, the warriors leapt into the circle. Flash moved round until the sun was behind his shoulder. As he circled them, the young men turned, like tall sunflowers following the course of the sun.

He did not need to tell them to smile: they were all smiling at the camera as they once had at their mothers, desperate to please.

Tchuck!

He used flash, to give himself the benefit of surprise. The warriors blinked, trying to be rid of the purple squares floating in their eyes. By the time they could see again, Flash was flapping the little square of cardboard to and fro between his fingers, like a god doing card tricks.

Second by second, grain by grain, they appeared, bunched together like thirteen marigolds in a pot, all with shy white smiles, all chosen as equal in worth by the just, wise, and all-seeing lens of the camera.

The Beauty

There was no such argument over which young woman Flash should photograph. The villagers brought her like a bride to his door: their greatest beauty.

'This is Finchow.'

Briefly (before his camera had nagged him to travel and see the world) Flash had taken photographs for magazines and shopping catalogues. He remembered the models who had trooped past his camera lens, leaning backwards from the hips, pouting their lips. He could picture them primping and prancing, spinning their skirts out wide. He could remember the young men, too, with gel in their hair, and child models the colour of corn. The beautiful people.

He remembered glimpsing girls on buses—so beautiful that he wanted to cry. He remembered film stars and famous TV faces and advertising hoardings ten metres high displaying gigantic beauties.

Now here was Finchow.

Of all the young women he had ever seen, Finchow was quite the . . . *ugliest*. True, her skin was smooth and velvety and she had a lot of hair. But then there was a lot of Finchow altogether. She towered over Flash, baring a ferocious jumble of teeth. Her plaits were braided with bunches of red lanka, her neck circled with big flat Frisbees of polished wood. The lobes of her ears stretched under the weight of earrings so heavy that the sight made Flash wince with pain.

She had been dusted with pollen, too: white like dandruff. Her clothing had been knotted the better to show off the width of her hips. Alarmed by the proud glare in her bulging eyes, Flash lowered his gaze. So he could not help noticing that her bare feet were bigger than his own were, even though he was wearing desert boots.

'Cinderella she ain't,' he said under his breath.

Then, turning to wink at Sutira, he saw his mistake. For Sutira was gazing at Finchow with exactly the wistful, wishful longing of a girl watching Cinderella dress for the ball. Here was everything Sutira wanted to be and never would—she with her slender, twiggy frame, her delicate hands and feet, her almond-shaped and praline-coloured eyes.

'Yesterday Finchow is a child,' said the Village Elder. 'Tomorrow she is old like us.

Today Finchow is a flower in bloom. The flower blossoms for such a little, little time.'

Flash dipped his head respectfully. 'I will photograph your beauty Finchow,' he said.

Well? If he could make a work-of-art out of a cow, he could make one of Finchow. It was easy. All he had to do was to look at her with their eyes. She was the turn-of-the-tide. She was the one-day lily.

He asked Finchow to stand against the pinks and lavenders of sunset, and framed the beauty in his viewfinder.

'Smile!'

And Finchow switched on the vain, self-satisfied smile of a supermodel, *knowing* she would be beautiful for ever. Flash almost envied her her foolishness.

Tchuck!

It was not until the picture appeared—second by second, grain by grain—that they

saw how, in the background, Flash had
managed to include a little girl playing in the
dirt, a bent old lady shielding her eyes from
the sun with knotty, arthritic hands.

'Myself, I think you are prettier,' he whispered to Sutira, as Finchow rushed hither and thither showing off her portrait to her many friends and admirers.

Sutira stared at him as if he was mad.

Flashman

Flash began to feel quite pleased with himself. He had brought joy and excitement to a corner of the world untouched before by the magic of photography. The villagers seemed to prize a guest singed by fire and magic. The old men offered him a variety of awful things to smoke and drink, while their wives were in a frenzy to feed him their cooking. The young women giggled and dropped their eyes when he passed. The young warriors were openly hostile (which was a bit scary but flattering). The women working among the lanka trees would shout saucy remarks as he walked the ravine each morning, savouring the light, and though he never caught what they said, it felt friendly—like someone tossing an apple to you out of a tree.

But as the days went by and his injuries healed, Flash feared he was giving photography a bad name. They must be thinking it such an easy, lazy kind of work in comparison with beating lanka bark, weaving, or pulping fruit. So he tried to lend a hand.

First, he began grooming the cow—but the cowherd came at a run and hauled him away. Perhaps she thought he would sour the milk.

So he took a few strips of bark and began beating them with a rock. The women's horrified stares were so unnerving that he brought the rock down on his own fingers. They shooed him away like a chicken. With his fingers tucked into his armpits, he even looked like a chicken.

He thought of sweeping the dog mess off the village pathways, but the noonday heat drove him back to the shade of the trees.

They were putting on their last flush of fruit before the dead season. Soft and luscious, the flesh formed inside a hard red peel that had to be cracked open and scooped out. So Flash sat down cross-legged under a tree, gathered a mound of fruit into his lap and began to crack the scarlet rinds carefully and deliberately. Like scarlet lacquer, the shell crazed. It was beautiful. The greenish, custardy mush inside spilled out between his knuckles and filled his lap with the savour of sprouts.

When he looked up, the entire village had mustered to stare at him—all shocked, all appalled, except for the warriors and children whose shoulders were jumping with laughter. Olu was rolling on the ground, laughing too hard to stand, pointing at the absurd sight of a man doing women's work.

Sutira slapped her little brother. Then she held one small hand in the air, demanding to be heard. *'Tomorrow Flash goes hunting!'* she announced in her most decided voice. 'Flash is a *mighty* hunter!'

Flash looked up into the treetops. The sun pierced the canopy like a thousand extremely sharp hunting spears. He considered explaining that he had never shot anything (unless you count pictures). He considered telling them he had once joined a protest against fox-hunting. He thought about giant lizards and edible grubs and skinning things, and considered saying he was a vegetarian. But when he lowered his gaze, Sutira was still looking at him, eyes narrowed, relying on him to be

Nimrod the Mighty Hunter.

'Grand,' he said. 'A hunt. Tomorrow. Just the thing.'

Unfortunately this caused an even worse commotion. The warriors looked crestfallen. The harvesters threw up their hands in sorrowful gestures that spilled armfuls of fruit around Flash's feet. The old women fluttered and puttered and pined.

'Oh, please . . .' said Sutira's mother, embracing her daughter fondly from behind and placing her hand firmly over the girl's mouth. 'Not tomorrow . . . Another day . . .'

Only the Village Elder dared to break the bad news to Flash. 'I regret tomorrow we ask you not to hunt. Our young men must be here. Our guest must be here. Today our harvest is in. Tomorrow comes the Feast of Final Fruits.'

Flash tried very, very hard to look disappointed.

He had not been going to take his camera to the Feast. But then he was afraid to leave it in the hut, for fear someone help themselves to one of his few remaining shots. So he slung it round his neck, like a big badge of office.

Then the women came from their huts with big shiny bowls full of peppers and peas, fruit and bakemeats, honeycombs, custards and stews, and unrolled stripy lanka matting and set their children on guard over the bowls, with fly swats. The air was multi-coloured with smells. The village gathered around the food, and the colours of evening gathered behind them. So picturesque!

They led him, as guest-of-honour, to the head of the ground-cloth. Olu and Sutira (who were not allowed so high) sat further down, sharing his jacket, each with one arm down one sleeve, to show he still belonged to them. A procession of harvesters circled the 'table' with a bowl of liquor distilled from the final fruits of the harvest. Too picturesque to resist!

'Smile everyone!'

Tchuck.

He had never liked sprouts. But there they stood at his shoulder, offering him the sprouty smell, offering him the processional bowl of liquor. One glance at Olu and Sutira, and Flash knew: to refuse would be to give offence. The bowl was a mark of honour and esteem.

So, taking a very deep breath, he put his lips to the rim, told his tongue to take cover, and swallowed down the entire contents of the bowl in a single nauseating gulp.

A gasp of wonder rippled like a fringe around the lanka matting. He looked up in time to see the warriors' jaws drop in awe and admiration, the harvester women wide-eyed with wonderment. He saw Olu and

Sutira hug the two cuffs of his jacket to their mouths in astonishment.

Always before: a single sip and then the cup had passed on. Always before. But Flash was such a formidable man that he had swallowed down the entire loving bowl! No wonder he could shake pictures from the tips of his fingers!

About one second after Flash realized his mistake, the trees suddenly spewed volcanic lava into the sky. The dogs grew seven metres tall and the huts were flying saucers speeding dangerously low over his head. The villagers' faces melted into surf washing to and fro around a stripey beach, and the bowls of food began moving around like giant land crabs. He was sure the music was real: he had never heard sweeter. He was certain he had never danced so well in his life.

But when he woke up, Olu and Sutira told

him he had not danced at all—simply stood very still, all evening, his back to a tree, without blinking, waiting for the perfect moment.

'What moment?' said Flash, warily. His memory was a blank.

Olu pointed to the camera around Flash's neck. It had poked out its tongue of card long before, and yet no one had presumed to pull it free for a closer look. No one had rifled through his clothing to find his photograph of the Feast. They had simply waited, in agonies of excitement, for the photographer to wake and give them their next two cardboard seconds snipped from Time.

Three days they had had to wait.

Flash looked at the latest photograph with curiosity. Since he had no recollection of taking it, it was like looking at another photographer's work. But it was a good

picture—the entire village dancing and singing through the firelight of a bonfire.

And he was glad he had taken his camera along, glad he had expended two precious photographs on the Feast of Final Fruits and on the Dance. Now, when the villagers' stomachs were empty and their mouths dry, when times were hard or disease blighted the fields, there would still be the photograph of those steaming bowls, those extravagant piles of peas and peppers.

Now, whenever there was grief or trouble or hardship, they could look at the photograph of themselves dancing and laughing and singing, and remember being cheerful.

(In as far as you can remember heat in the winter or cold in the summer.)

The subject of hunting did not arise again. The warriors were too much in awe of Flash to pit their puny skills against his, whether in hunting, drinking, or sleeping.

Fading Away

'Our pictures. They fade.'

Flash's heart missed a beat. He knew, of course, that instant pictures do not stay as bright as ordinary photos. But he had not expected them to fade so soon. 'Tell everyone: they must keep them out of the sunlight!' he urged Olu.

Olu looked at him quizzically, head on one side. 'How?'

The pictures Olu was really talking about were painted on a pillar of rock fifty metres high, a kilometre or so from the village. It was impossible to tell how long they had weathered the blazing sun, the rare outbursts of rain, the blast of blowing sand: one thousand years, perhaps two.

Ancestors of the villagers had ground their paint out of berry juice, blood, and mineral pigments. Perhaps one, perhaps two thousand years before, they had walked up from the village and ringed this huge finger of rock with hand prints, cattle, running figures, symbols, and patterns. Back then, their pictures must have been a riot of reds and blues and yellows. Now they were almost as faint as pencil sketches.

The sight of the ancestral paintings set Flash's imagination reeling: the thought of the men and women who had painted them, making their mark, making themselves immortal by painting scenes from their everyday lives. How many generations had stood and gazed at this frieze of pictures and patterns? The rock itself was so big it would never wear away—not while humans inhabited the earth, anyway. The paintings, on the other hand, were nearing the end of their long, long life, worn away by sun and rain, frost and wind, but most of all by the touch of countless human hands admiring their beauty.

'Paint ancestors' pictures,' said the village artist, pointing to Flash's camera. Small and skinny, the artist himself looked like one of the stick figures worn faint by touching. 'Then, when they are gone, we still have your magic painting!'

Flash looked down at his flimsy, plastic box of tricks. He recalled Sutira's words when he had told her that cameras 'took pictures': *'Can't take ours,'* she had said. *'We need them.'*

'Oh, but photographs are *nothing*,' he said

helplessly. 'Alongside this rock, photographs are nothing!'

Photographs fade. Photographs tear. Photographs mildew and curl and go brown. Heat crazes their glaze. Ants destroy them. Before Sutira or Olu were even as old as the Village Elder, Flash's foolish, useless little photographs would be unreadable. The food pictured in 'The Feast' would be blotched with brown, like mould. The figures in 'The Dance' would be white ghosts haunting a white wilderness.

'I'm sorry! Photographs last such a little, little while!' he told the village artist, pleading for forgiveness. He started to say, 'Why don't you repaint the rock yourselves?' But he had no sooner begun than he stopped. You do not touch up a painting by Michelangelo, or darn the Bayeux Tapestry, or mend the Venus de Milo with Polyfilla. 'Of course I will photograph your painting,' he said despairingly, 'but it's not enough!'

The artist gave such a beaming smile that Flash wanted to capture it on film. He looked at the back of the camera. Only four shots remained.

So he waited and watched for a whole day—from first light until the sun sank—to see in what light the ancestral paintings stood out best against their custard-coloured rock. Finding that the evening light was best, he waited another day round, to take the very best picture he could. He even built a cairn of rocks in place of a tripod, so that the camera would not shake so much as a hair's breadth when he pressed the button.

The painted pictures bounded exuberantly all around the rock. The photograph he took showed only one small section of one rockface. In the viewfinder of the camera, a gang of stick figures chased after a pig, while women stood surrounded by children and cooking pots. What he had at first mistaken for a weeping person with many arms proved to be a tree dripping its liquor and shedding its bark for lanka. The pattern of life had been repeating itself here for more years than Flash could possibly hold in his imagination.

Tchuck.

'He is doing reverence to the Ancestors,' said the people of the village, seeing how long Flash spent up by the painted rock. But, on the contrary, Flash was feeling only shame, as the small, inadequate picture flapped, drying, between his fingers. To think that he—a mere photographer— should be entrusted with preserving a true work of art!

The Moon
and Tixa

If you look at a photograph of the full moon at its zenith, and around it the flocking constellations, you will be looking at a code. Only from one point on the Earth's vast surface could that picture have been taken. Only from one spot will moon and stars look just so.

Grain by grain, hour by hour, the idea appeared in Flash's head like an instant print developing. If he were to photograph the moon and stars and then find his way back to civilization, he would be able to show his photo to an astronomer and discover the precise position of this remote and secret place.

He would be able to return! To preserve the paintings on the rock on slow-speed film with sun-filters, or on a digital camera using a hundred-thousand pixels, or on moving film! He would be able to photograph the conical huts and fermenting fruit, the peculiar brown of the children's eyes. He would take shots of his aeroplane's three seats which now stood on a wooden platform, like kingly thrones. At sunset the young men slumped in them, drinking liquor and pretending to keep look-out; during the day, birds plucked stuffing out through slits in the leather.

He would photograph the ravine walls—lavender in the early morning, powder-blue in full sun, and pink in the evenings. He would photograph the women at work weaving, the dogs sleeping in the pools of shadow around each hut.

And all he needed, to be able to pinpoint this valley hidden from Time and Civilization, was one shot of the full moon cloaked round with stars. After all, he was entitled to one shot out of the ten . . . As he said to Olu: 'It's my camera!'

Olu and Sutira followed him everywhere. They had sat with him at the foot of the painted rock. Now they walked with him under the night sky, pointing out the warriors and lizards and lanka trees formed by the clustering stars. (The villagers, too, looked to the night sky so as to know their place on Earth.)

'What next? What next? What is the next picture?' they kept asking. 'The lanka braids? The new thatch? The goat killing?'

Flash lay on his back on the ground and tried to shut out their shrill little voices. 'Not important,' he told them or, 'Unphotographable.'

'Why photograph that? It will be the same next year and the year after . . . ?'

The viewfinder of the camera was cloudy with condensation: it was the hour of dewfall. He wiped it with his shirt cuff. Over his head the full moon was a huge silver gong vibrating. The stars were needle sharp.

For the astrological calculation to work, he must catch the moon at its very highest point, before it began its slide back down the sky. A half-hour wait, he estimated. He must include the Pole Star, too, in the picture. It was part of the Science. Through the viewfinder he could see the dark seas on the moon's pitted surface, like age-spots on an old person's face. The ground under his back was hard and lumpy. Stones dug into his back. Not long now.

'You paint lanka braids,' said Sutira. 'That

way we can show them at market when none left.'

'You paint the Head of Village,' said Olu. 'He remembers the war.'

Flash checked the back of the camera, though he knew perfectly well how many prints were left. 'I haven't forgotten him,' he said sharply.

'You paint my dog,' said Sutira. 'Best dog in the whole world.'

Through his viewfinder, the code wrote itself on the night sky: the code that would let Flash find his way back to Paradise. The only question was, could the instant camera see well enough in the dark? You cannot use flash to capture the stars.

'Why you paint the moon?' said Olu who was lying on his back, his head in the angle of Flash's armpit.

'Well, I . . .' But it was too complicated to

explain. These were simple, primitive children. How could they possibly understand about navigation and astronomy and geomathematics?

'The moon comes back. Don't you worry,' said Sutira, lying on the other side of him, soothingly stroking his hair. 'It grows big. It grows small. It goes. But every time it comes back. We have no fear.' Then she explained to Olu how some superstitious people (like Flash) lived in fear of the moon shrinking out of existence and never reappearing.

''S all right, mister,' said Olu. 'Moon always comes back. God is good. Don't need to paint the moon. Truly!' He could hear the pleading in their voices: *Don't waste our magic on the moon! Poor, ignorant, superstitious sap*, they were thinking.

Above him, the white-faced moon reached its zenith. The landscape was hardly darker now than by day—just robbed of all its colour. In the moonlight, Flash could clearly see a circle of shadowy figures watching him from a distance. For one frightening moment he thought he must be seeing the ancestors mustering in ghostly regiments. Then he realized that the whole village was shadowing his movements, watching and waiting to see how he would spend his last precious pictures; which of their requests would be answered.

'When I come back,' he began to say, 'I can photograph *everything*! Anything you want!'

He could hear that his voice was wheedling and whiny. But why should he make excuses for using his own camera? Why should he apologize for photographing the moon?

Quickly, resolutely, he lay back and rested the camera over his face, fumbling for the button before the moon passed its zenith. A scarf of cloud, purple and silken, was drifting across the sky, threatening to cover the stars. He had to be quick . . .

'Tixa won't come back,' said Sutira.

'Tixa? What's Tixa?'

'My cousin. Tixa. She has wilting sickness. Be gone tomorrow.'

'Gone?'

'Gone.'

Flash watched the purple scarf of cloud ruffle and billow across the glittering sky. Like ink spilling across a map, first it blotted out the Pole Star, then the constellation of Cassiopeia. Through the back of his head he could feel the tiny vibration of fifty people stepping restlessly from foot to foot.

Painfully, Flash stood up. 'No arguments!' he called loudly to all the gathered villagers. 'I will paint Sutira's cousin Tixa!'

Flash ran all the way. He half hoped Tixa would be asleep. But he was glad when she was not. She had Sutira's almond-shaped eyes and they looked huge in her pale and pinched little face. She was so ill, so close to death, that he did not expect her to know who he was. But she did. So too did her mother, grasping him by the sleeve, patting his hand.

Tchuck!

But when he took the photo—*'Rubbishy, cheap cameras!'*—there was no explosion of light. His groping fingertips found no flash-cube on the corner of the casing. It must have fallen off the camera as he ran, or when he brushed through the flyscreen at the door of the hut. By the light of the single candle burning, he stood no chance of finding it. The camera stuck out its tongue of white card, but he knew that it held nothing but the promise of darkness.

'*There's not enough light! There's not enough light!*' cried Flash, panic-stricken. Morning was still far off and his camera had spewed out nothing but a picture of darkness. However you looked at it, Tixa—lovely little Tixa—was leaving behind in the world nothing but a dark

space. The thought was unbearable.

Luckily, the villagers did not share his panic. They simply picked up Tixa, cot and all, and carried her outside. Then they lit branches wrapped in lanka—dozen upon dozens of flaming torches—and placed themselves around her: human arc lamps in a midnight studio. Brightest of all was the full moon overhead—a big white lamp sprinkling the ground with dapple.

Smile? thought Flash. Hardly. How could he ask it? There was nothing to smile about here.

Fortunately the villagers had grown used to the magic words of photography. '*SMILE!*' they shouted, in one great roar as bright as the firelight. Flames danced in the little girl's almond-shaped eyes, and then the eyes wrinkled away to slits as she gave the biggest, prettiest smile Flash had ever seen.

Tixa smiled again when she saw herself—fire-gilded and moon-lit—beaming out from the little square of card.

Tixa left the village with the set of the moon. Over her empty bed her photo hung from a strip of cloth (to save it from the

insects). Flash could find no comfort in seeing it there—no, not one shred—but the village seemed to think differently.

Never before had the Dead continued to smile in the land of the Living.

However hard you try to remember a face, it slips, little by little, out of the memory. It fades, year by year, grain by grain, into oblivion. Not Tixa's. Thanks to the photograph, her smile would be seen by children not yet born, and still remembered after a thousand moons had risen and set.

Smile!

'And after that I want to photograph each of the bridges over the Thames—not just the bridge but the people who use it, the different people who cross over and pass under . . . I want to shoot the City at night— all the delivery vans—people hosing down the streets—the fluffers cleaning the human hair off the Underground rails while the electricity is off . . .'

Seated around the feast they had prepared in honour of the magician, the villagers smiled back at him and nodded. Nothing he said made one word of sense to them. He knew it. He was describing a world they had never seen: one that would never even brush its skirts against theirs. And yet his head was so teeming with ideas that he had to talk about them.

'. . . And I want to do a book of Opposites! Full-page art photos side-by-side: happy-sad, rich-poor, old and young, wet and dry, war and peace, the Arctic and the tropics . . .'

As soon as the last of his ten photographs was taken, he would set off on the long trek back to civilization. Flash wanted these people to know that there would be more photographs, better photographs . . .

' . . . I want to record the whole of a Life—from the newborn to the deathbed! Ninety-six pages and no text. Not one word!' (Flash has never been at ease with words; only pictures.)

The villagers smiled and nodded, nodded and smiled, affectionately. At one point, Olu brought him something small, on the flat of his hand, and Flash took it between finger and thumb, thinking it was a tasty morsel. It was halfway to his mouth before he realized it was the flash-cube from his camera. Olu and Sutira had scoured the wilderness until they found it.

'And now I want to paint *you*, sir,' Flash told the old, old man. 'Naturally I saved the last picture for the most important person: the Village Elder.' He relished the idea of capturing those deeply wrinkled cheeks, those milky blue eyes, the white stubble of that loose-skinned jaw. The Village Elder looked like some biblical prophet or legendary king.

But to his surprise, the old, old man rocked his heavy head to and fro between his bony shoulders. 'No. I have no wish for such a painting.'

Flash felt almost offended. 'Why?'

The Elder waved a large, slow, maimed hand in front of his face, disturbing the flies. 'A man changes with time,' he said. 'He grows up. He grows wiser. He grows older. Sometimes old age is a big price to buy wisdom. Once I was a young man—like those foolish warriors you paint. Once I was strong and fit. And handsome—hard to believe, I know! The young women then, they breathe deeper when I pass by. Glad to slip a hand into mine . . .' He studied the lopped, crooked hands that lay spread in his lap. 'When I die, the people will look back. Then the years of my old age will be no more seen than the years of my youth, the years of my manhood. My short temper, my lame leg, my no-teeth smile: soon all these will be forgotten, and I will be a man of all ages and no age. I will be all the good parts. I will be my name and my deeds and not this face-inruins. But, Mr Flash, if you paint my picture with your camera, I will be for ever an old man. If you picture me, I am for ever old. Ask your aeroplane, Mr Flash. How wants your aeroplane to be remembered? Heap of burned metal? Or bird in the sky?'

Flash put back the lens cap, wrapped the cord around the camera, and set it aside.

' . . . I do have a wish, naturally,' said the old, old man. 'There is a picture I *do* want you to paint.'

Flash picked up the camera again. 'Name it.'

'I wish for a picture of the man who fell from the sky. I want a picture of you.'

Flash had stood behind many cameras— camcorders and infra-red; rapid-action and time-delay; reflex-lens, glass-plate, digital, and panoramic. But never before had anyone asked to take *his* photograph. Never before and never again would anyone pin his photo to a strip of cloth (to save it from the insects) and point it out with pride and say: *This is the magician who fell from the sky and gave us ten seconds to keep for ever*.

'It would be a waste of a shot!' Flash protested. 'I'm not useful like the cow! Or beautiful like Finchow! Or priceless like the paintings of your ancestors!'

'But soon you will be gone, like Tixa,' said the Village Elder. 'And when we sit in aeroplane seats and we speak the legend of the man fallen from the sky, it will be good to say: *Look, this is no lie. Here is the man. Here is the proof.*'

Next moment, the children descended, like a flock of colourful birds, and dragged Flash away from the feast, up the well trodden path to the ancestral paintings. His shadow, black in the strong sunlight, joined the dancing stick-figures painted on the rock.

They set the camera on the cairn of stones Flash had built as a tripod, and sprang from foot to foot, yelping and laughing as the old, old man made his unhurried way up the steep incline. To him must go the honour, of course, of taking the photographer's photograph.

'Smile!' said the Village Elder, with a crooked, boyish grin. One of his few remaining fingers hovered over the button.

But Flash did not smile.

'SMILE!' roared the crowd.

But Flash could not. In fact, the curve of his mouth turned down rather than up. 'I'm sorry. I can't remember how,' he apologized. 'I am too sad at the thought of leaving you all.'

The Last Flash

'So?' said the Village Elder. 'Stay.'
'Stay!' said Olu.

'Yes! Stay!' said Sutira.

Flash struggled to explain. But he had never been any good with words, only pictures. Suddenly he began to slap at his scorched and ragged jacket, feeling all the pockets for something of tremendous importance. Why had he not thought of it before? At last, with a gasp of relief, he drew out his wallet from an inside pocket, and from his wallet a little square of cardboard.

'I have to get back!' said Flash, and pushed at them the photograph that explained exactly why he could not stay. There was his beautiful wife, his three lovely children: a girl about Tixa's age, a boy the size of Olu, another about as old as Sutira.

The prized photograph was passed around from hand to hand. Each villager in turn studied it. Then their eyes would flick back to Flash—a look of pained sympathy. It took Finchow to put everyone's thoughts into words: 'Ugly woman!' she said, and shuddered as she put the photograph back into Flash's hand.

Then Flash remembered how to smile. In fact he leaned one hand against the painted rock—his hand covering a red handprint—and laughed out loud.

It would have made a great photograph. It would have pleased the ancestors—and the storytellers, too, who in times to come would tackle the legend of The Man who

Fell Out of the Sky.

Unfortunately, the big cheer that went up from the villagers startled Sutira's dog. It dashed through the forest of legs and brushed against the pile of rocks holding the camera. The rocks collapsed with a noisy rattle that scared the dog even more.

The camera tumbled down among the jumble of stones and its strap caught around the dog's neck. Finding itself banged and shunted by the camera, the dog ran faster. When the crowd began to chase it, the dog ran faster still.

A photographer's first thought is always for his camera. Flash took off after the dog and did not stop chasing it even when the villagers gave up. Even when the painted rock was no longer in sight—even when the camera, bouncing and clattering alongside the dog, flashed like a mirror breaking in the sun. The flash drove the dog to one last frantic effort, and it finally broke free, snapping the strap, sending the camera catapulting onwards in a cloud of dust.

Flash stumbled, his feet taken from under him by the dog bolting back the way it had come. He pitched over the edge of an escarpment he had not even seen.

They landed side by side, photographer and camera, and the camera poked out at him a jeering white tongue. Just as if he had drunk more of the women's bitter liquor, Flash found that his hands were out of use. He had no choice but to watch the square of paper as, second by second, grain by grain, it revealed to him the last picture on the film.

An expanse of sky. A brown muzzle. The triangle of an ear. It seemed to Flash that the children's dog was not so much smiling as grinning into the lens.

'Very clever. To use the camera. Very
ingenious. To signal us with the camera
flash. We'd never have found you otherwise.
You moved a long way from the crash site.'

His rescuer sounded chiding, like the mother of a child who has wilfully wandered off and lost itself. 'You really should have stayed by the plane.'

'Mark the co-ordinates on the map!' cried Flash seizing him by the wrist. 'The exact spot where you found me! There's a village near there! I have to find it again!'

The helicopter roared and rattled around him, a booming noise overlaid by the *tchuck, tchuck, tchuck* of the rotorblades.

'Village? In these parts? Hardly,' said the winch-man. 'Nothing but desert and landmines.'

Flash told them: 'A ravine, with lanka trees and a big painted rock fifty metres high!'

But if such trees existed, the search party had never heard of them. Besides, since the drought, there had been no trees of any kind—none for a hundred miles. 'And what language did they speak, then, these primitives? The Queen's English, was it?' said the pilot over his shoulder, snorting with laughter at the wild nonsense Flash was talking.

In the heat, the piece of cardboard in Flash's hand had become so tacky that it had stuck to his palm. Even the down-draught of the landing helicopter had not dislodged it. Now, as he tugged it free, the surface peeled away in patches—the blue of the sky, the dog's ear, the black fleck of something that might be an approaching aircraft . . .

Flash sat up and looked around him at the vibrating steel floor with its litter of equipment, winches, and first-aid. 'In the plane . . . were there seats? Were the three seats still in the plane when you found it? There weren't any seats, were there?'

'Couldn't tell you,' said the winch-man with a shrug. 'Everything burned. Whole plane was gutted. Take it easy now.'

'What about my camera?'

'There was a fireproof box of kit in the crash. We salvaged that. With any luck your cameras will be—'

'No, no! Not them! The instant-print one! The one I had with me! The instant one!'

The pilot officer sucked his teeth. 'Sorry,' he said. 'We didn't bother to bring it.' Seeing Flash's face fall, he added, 'Those things are cheap enough, aren't they? I've got one. Surprised you even use one, a professional like you . . .'

Finchow. Olu. Sutira. Tixa and the cow. Flash spoke their names, thinking aloud. Was it possible that they had never even existed outside his head?

''Sides . . . you must have used the film up

before your plane went down,' the winch-man went on. 'There were no prints left. I looked. Not a one.'

Flash rested his aching head back on the steel floor and felt his teeth chatter with the vibration of the aircraft. '*That's* all right, then!' he said with a great sigh of relief. '*That's* all right!'

And he closed his eyes and allowed himself the luxury of a smile.